NURSERY RHYMES FROM
MOTHER GOOSE

Harry Bornstein and Karen L. Saulnier

Illustrated by Patricia Peters
Line Drawings by Linda C. Tom

Kendall Green Publications
Gallaudet University Press

TOLD IN SIGNED ENGLISH

Kendall Green Publications

An imprint of Gallaudet University Press
Washington, DC 20002-3695

Book design by Sharon Davis Thorpe, Panache Designs

Library of Congress Cataloging-in-Publication Data

Bornstein, Harry.
  Nursery rhymes from Mother Goose (told in Signed English) / Harry
Bornstein and Karen L. Saulnier; illustrated by Pat Peters; sign illustrated
by Linda Tom.
    p. cm.
  Summary: Presents well-known Mother Goose rhymes accompanied by
diagrams showing how to form the Signed English signs for each word in
the poems.
  ISBN 0-930323-99-8
  1. Nursery rhymes.   2. Children's poetry.   3. American Sign Language.
[1. Nursery rhymes.   2. Sign language.]   I. Saulnier, Karen Luczak.
II. Peters, Pat, ill.   III. Tom, Linda C., ill.
IV. Title.
PZ8.B6485Nu 1992
398.8—dc20   91-42409
                                                                    CIP
                                                                    AC

Preface

Signed English is a communication system that allows its users to simultaneously say and sign the patterns of spoken English. Its manual component is based on American Sign Language, but includes invented signs and grammatical sign "markers." When properly implemented, Signed English provides an English-language environment in which hard-of-hearing and other language-delayed children can learn the vocabulary and structure of English. In Signed English, each sign corresponds to one English word. Words that cannot be represented by signs can be fingerspelled using the American Manual Alphabet.

Signed English was designed to be used with speech. Hard-of-hearing children learn English through a combination of hearing spoken words, speechreading, and seeing manual signs.

Nursery Rhymes From Mother Goose Told in Signed English makes well-known nursery rhymes accessible to hard-of-hearing children in a new and inviting way. Read the nursery rhymes aloud to your child. Learn the signs so that you can read and sign the nursery rhymes at the same time. This will help your child to associate specific signs with specific English words and lip movements. Encourage your child to repeat the signs and words and to recite the nursery rhymes.

Many other stories and books are available in the Signed English Series. For more information, contact **Gallaudet University Press**.

American Manual Alphabet

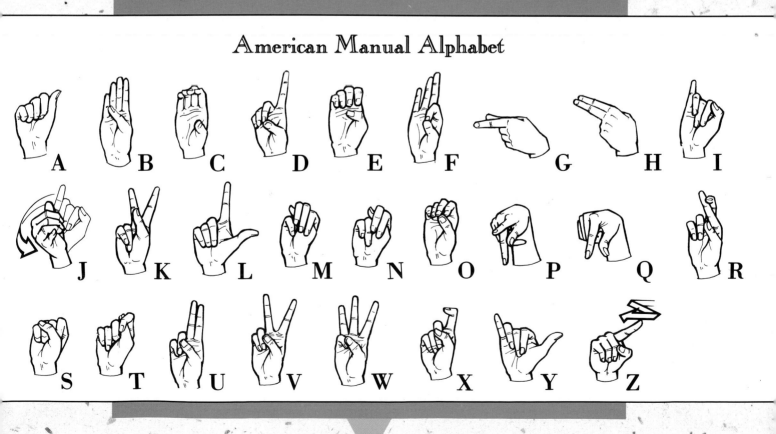

CONTENTS

HUMPTY DUMPTY

Humpty Dumpty sat on a wall,
Humpty Dumpty had a great fall;
All the King's horses and all the King's men

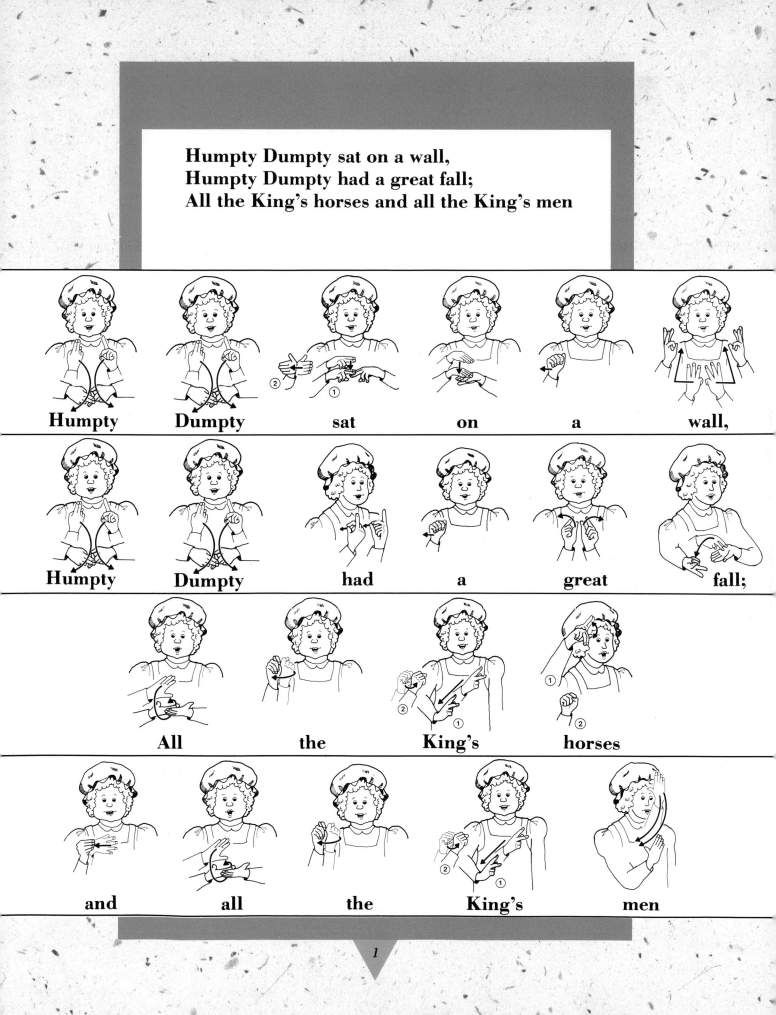

| Humpty | Dumpty | sat | on | a | wall, |

| Humpty | Dumpty | had | a | great | fall; |

| All | the | King's | horses |

| and | all | the | King's | men |

Couldn't put Humpty together again.

Couldn't   put   Humpty   together   again.

BAA, BAA, BLACK SHEEP

Baa, baa, black sheep,
  Have you any wool?
Yes, sir, yes, sir,
  Three bags full;

Baa, baa,	black	sheep,	Have	you	any	wool?

Yes,	sir,	yes,	sir,	Three	bags	full;

One for my master,
One for my dame,
And one for the little boy
Who lives in our lane.

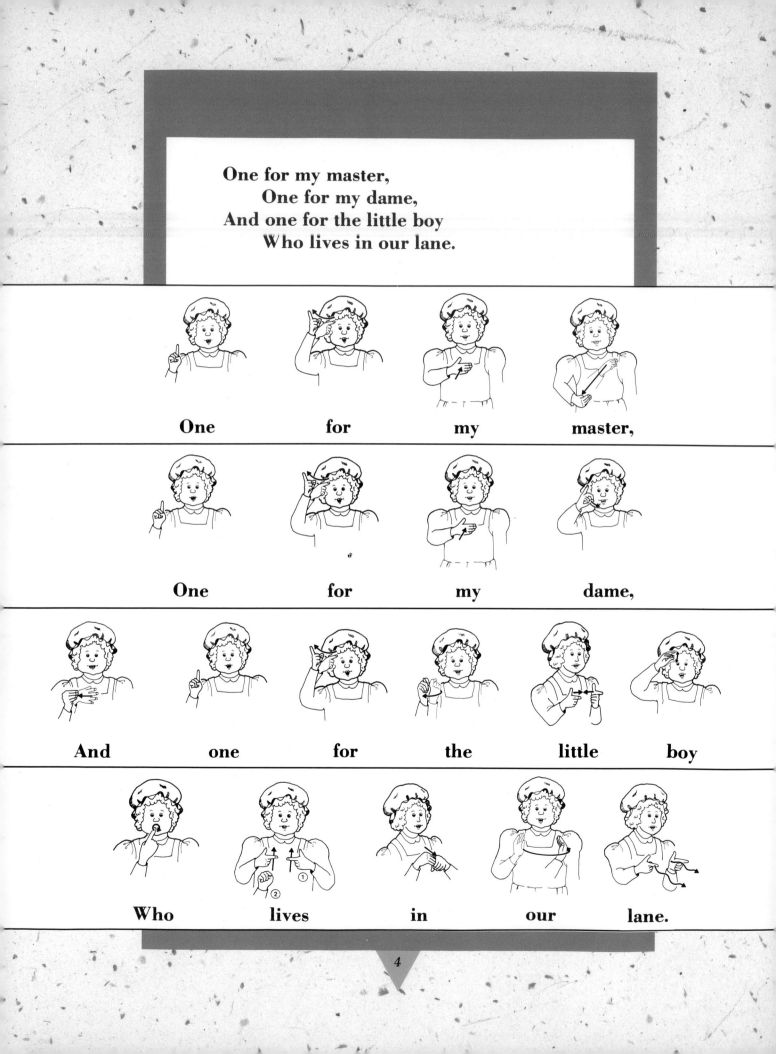

| One | for | my | master, |

| One | for | my | dame, |

| And | one | for | the | little | boy |

| Who | lives | in | our | lane. |

5

FIVE LITTLE PIGS

This little pig went to market;
This little pig stayed home;
This little pig had roast beef;
This little pig had none;

This   little   pig   went   to   market;

This   little   pig   stayed   home;

This   little   pig   had   roast   beef;

This   little   pig   had   none;

This little pig cried, "Wee, wee, wee,"
All the way home.

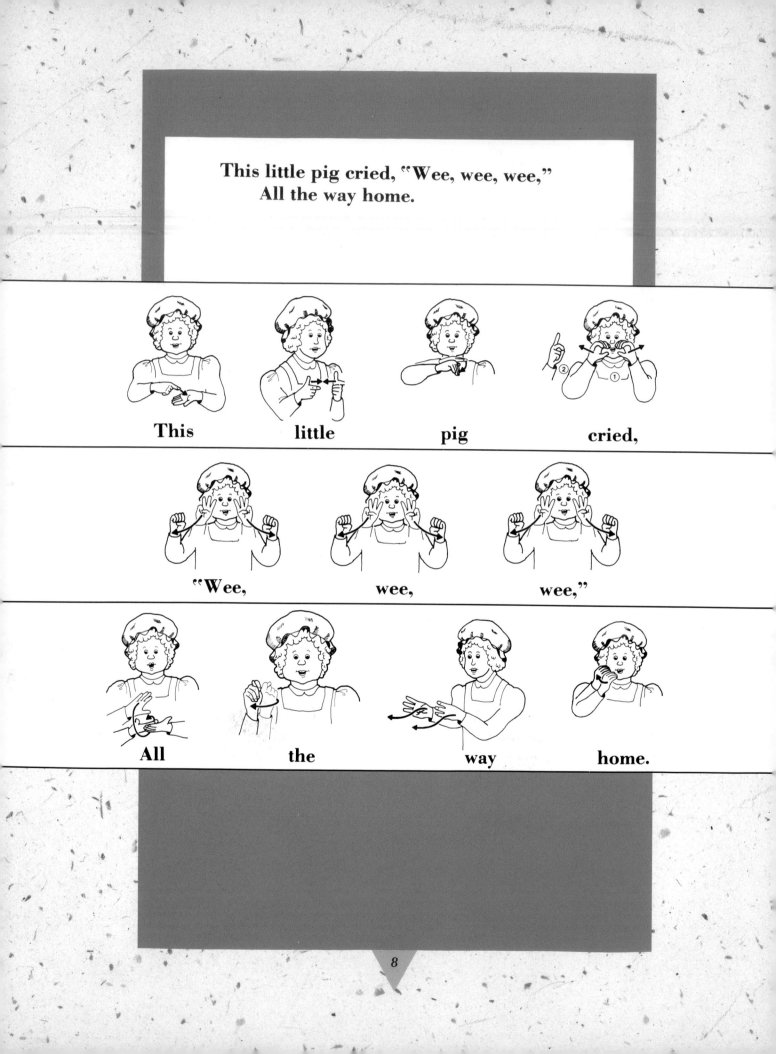

This   **little**   **pig**   **cried,**

"Wee,   **wee,**   **wee,"**

All   **the**   **way**   **home.**

LITTLE BO-PEEP

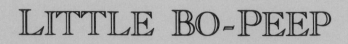

Little Bo-Peep has lost her sheep,
And can't tell where to find them;

Little	Bo-	Peep	has	lost	her	sheep,

And	can't	tell	where	to	find	them;

Leave them alone, and they'll come home,
Wagging their tails behind them.

Leave   them   alone,   and   they'll   come   home,

Wagging   their   tails   behind   them.

PAT-A-CAKE

Pat-a-cake, pat-a-cake, baker's man!
Bake me a cake as fast as you can.

Pat-a-cake,   pat-a-cake,   baker's   man!

Bake   me   a   cake

as   fast   as   you   can.

Roll it and pat it and mark it with "B,"
Put it in the oven for Baby and me.

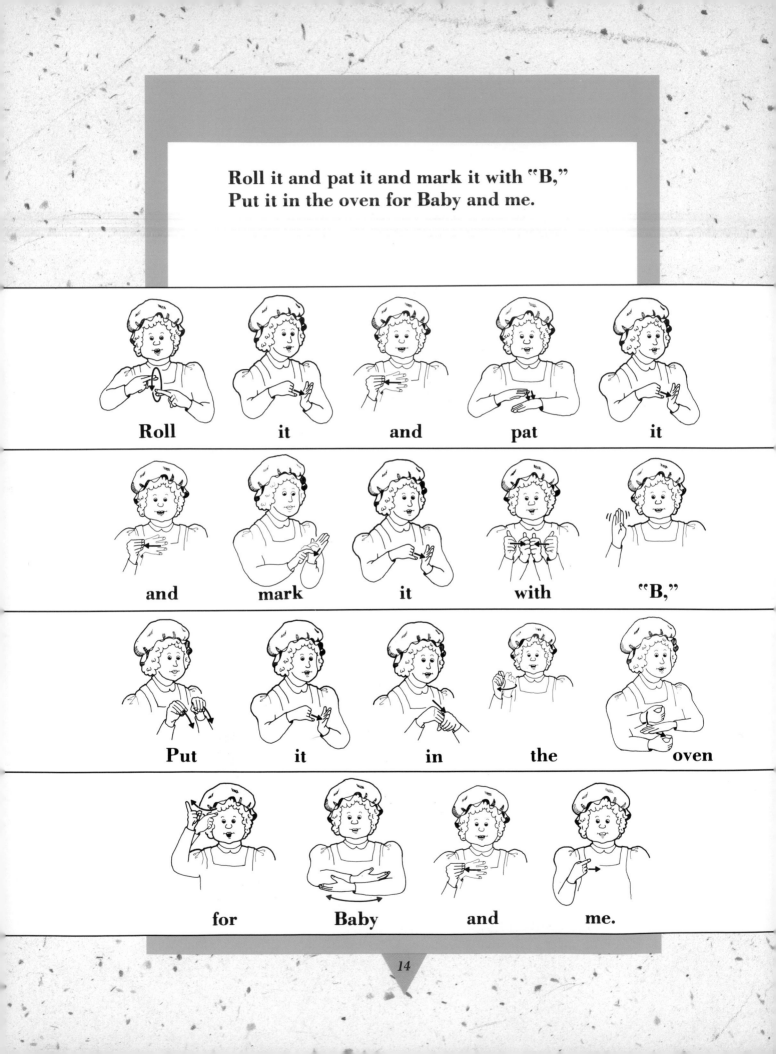

Little Boy Blue,
  Come blow your horn!
The sheep are in the meadow,
  The cows are in the corn.

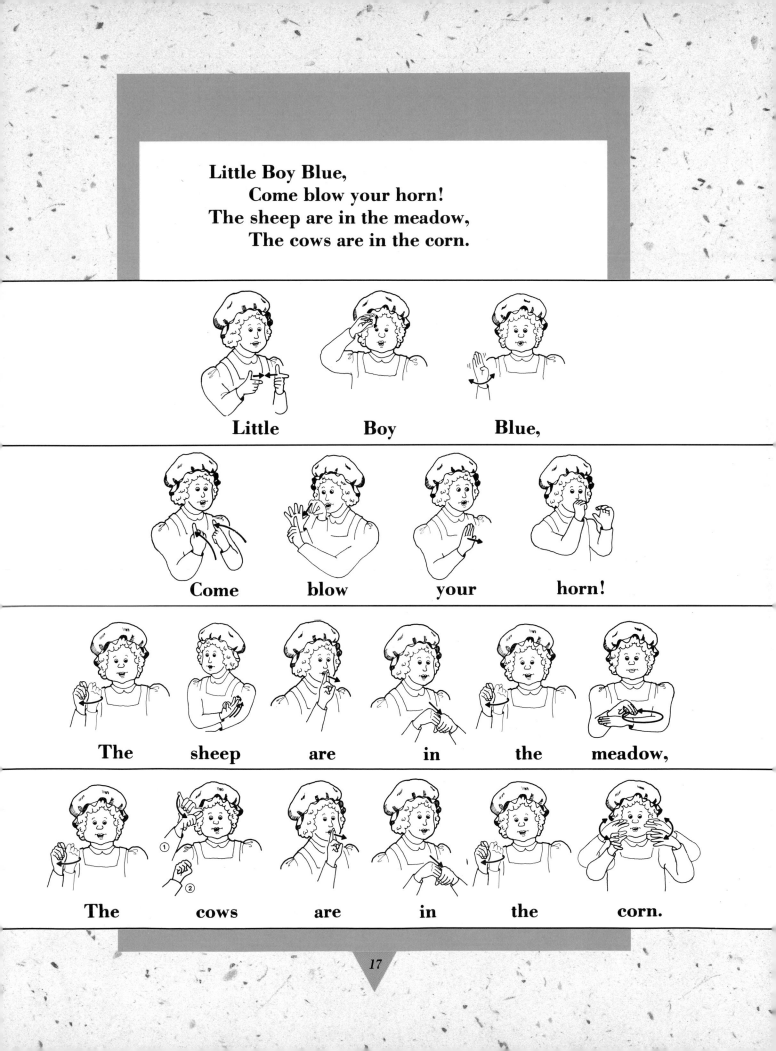

Little   **Boy**   **Blue,**

Come   **blow**   **your**   **horn!**

The   **sheep**   **are**   **in**   **the**   **meadow,**

The   **cows**   **are**   **in**   **the**   **corn.**

Where's the boy
    Who looks after the sheep?
He's under the haystack,
    Fast asleep.

Where's   the   boy

Who   looks   after   the   sheep?

He's   under   the   haystack,   Fast   asleep.

OLD MOTHER HUBBARD

Old Mother Hubbard
    Went to the cupboard,
To get her poor dog a bone;
When she got there
    The cupboard was bare,

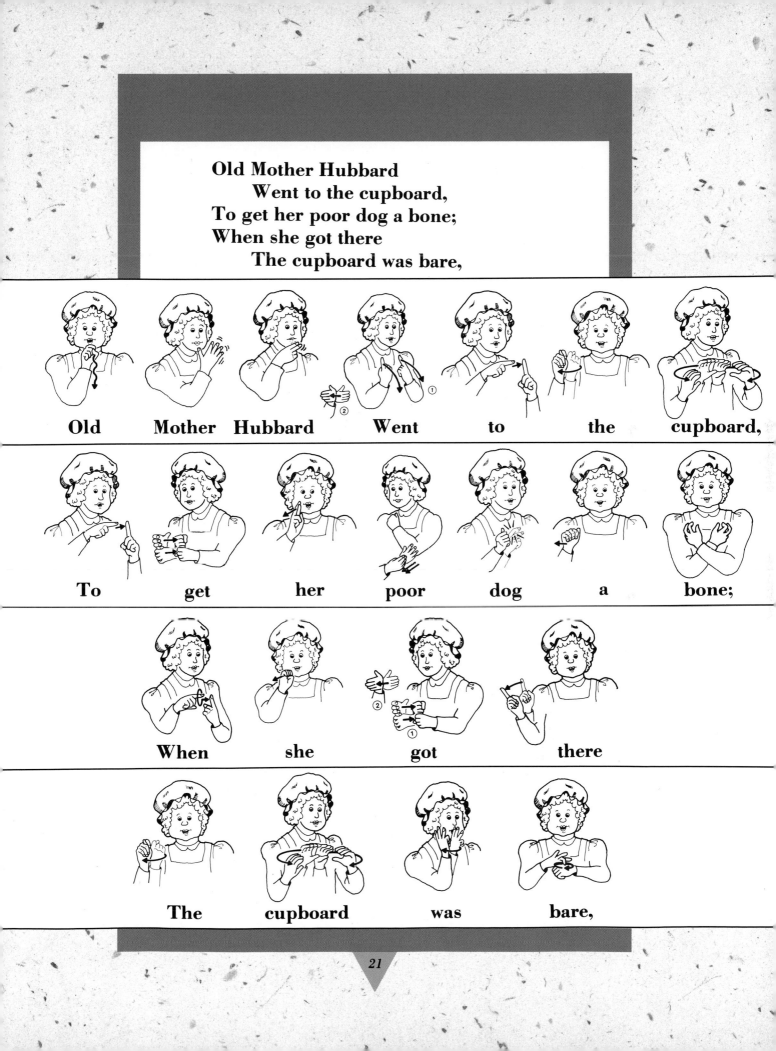

| Old | Mother | Hubbard | Went | to | the | cupboard, |

| To | get | her | poor | dog | a | bone; |

| When | she | got | there |

| The | cupboard | was | bare, |

And so the poor dog got none.

And **so** **the** **poor** **dog** **got** **none.**

THE CAT AND THE FIDDLE

Hey, diddle, diddle!
The cat and the fiddle,
The cow jumped over the moon;

Hey, diddle, diddle!

The   cat   and   the   fiddle,

The   cow   jumped   over   the   moon;

23

The little dog laughed
To see such sport,
And the dish ran away with the spoon.

The little dog laughed

To see such sport,

And the dish ran away

with the spoon.

LITTLE MISS MUFFET

Little Miss Muffet
Sat on a tuffet,
Eating her curds and whey;
Along came a spider,
Who sat down beside her,

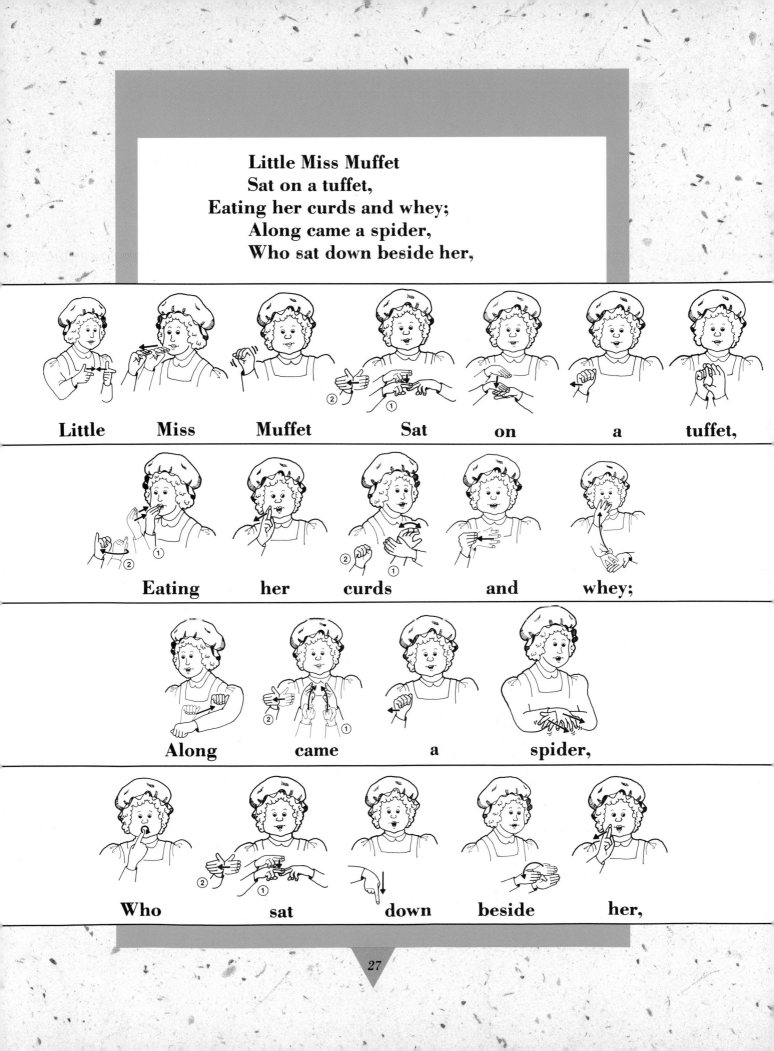

Little Miss Muffet Sat on a tuffet,

Eating her curds and whey;

Along came a spider,

Who sat down beside her,

And frightened Miss Muffet away.

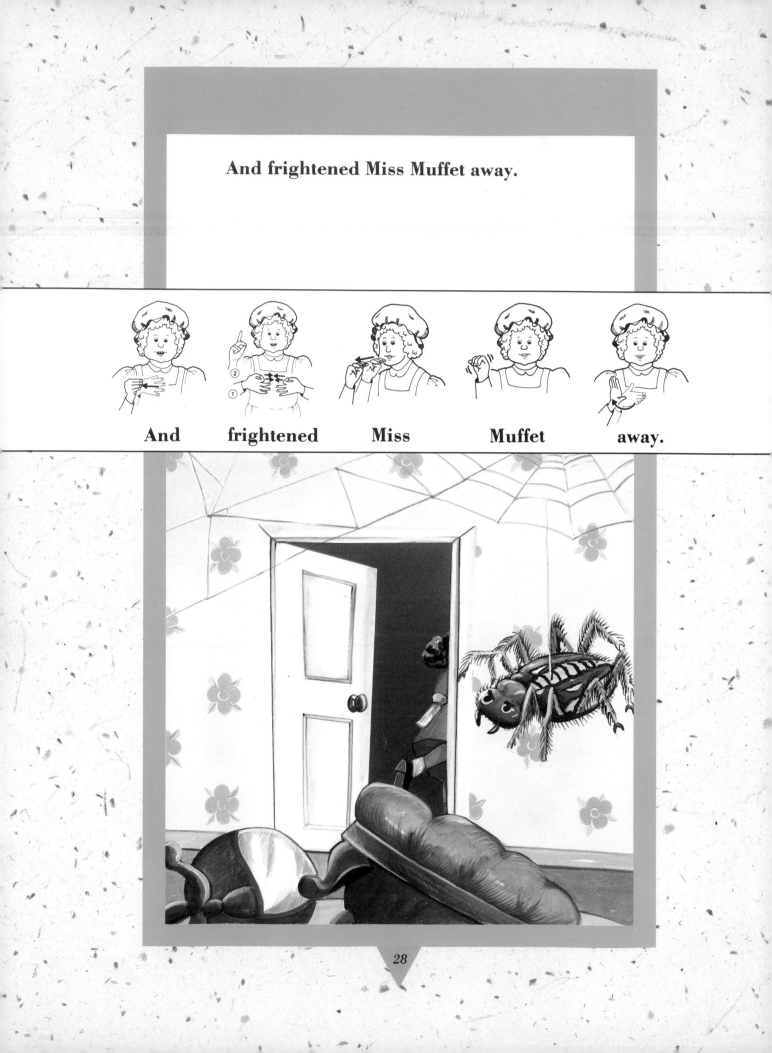

And frightened Miss Muffet away.

28

LITTLE JACK HORNER

Little Jack Horner
Sat in a corner,
Eating a Christmas pie;

Little	Jack	Horner

Sat	in	a	corner,

Eating	a	Christmas	pie;

29

He put in his thumb,
And pulled out a plum,
And said, "What a good boy am I!"

He   put   in   his   thumb,

And   pulled   out   a   plum,

And   said,   "What   a

good   boy   am   I!"

MARY HAD A LITTLE LAMB

Mary had a little lamb,
  Its fleece was white as snow;
And everywhere that Mary went,
  The lamb was sure to go.

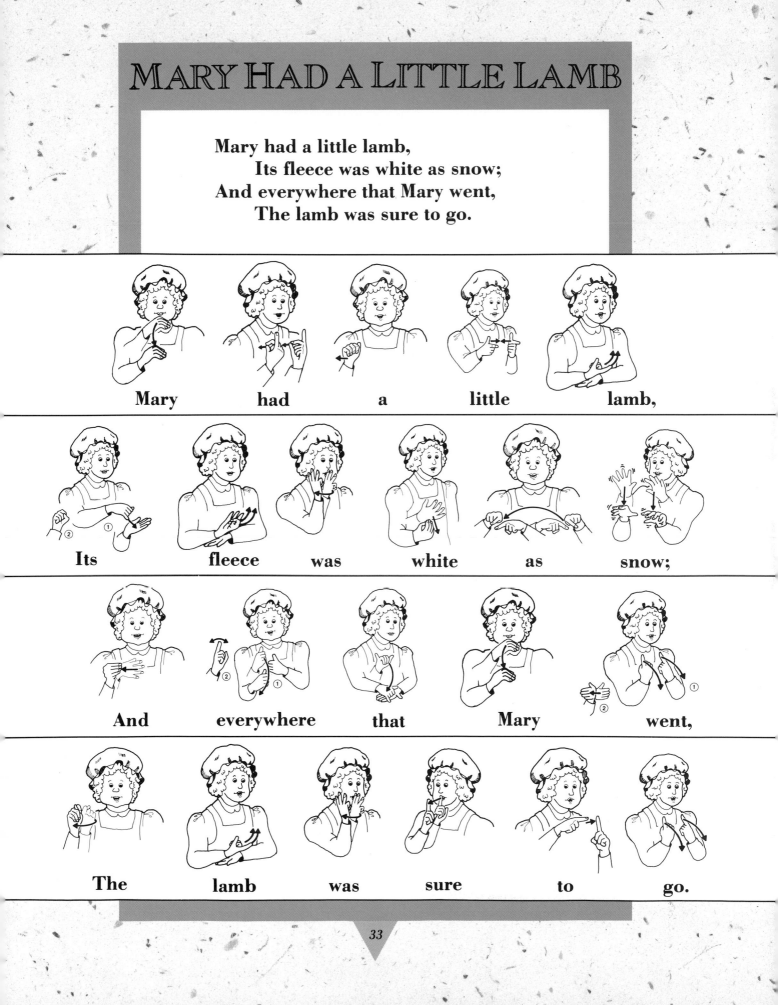

Mary had a little lamb,

Its fleece was white as snow;

And everywhere that Mary went,

The lamb was sure to go.

It followed her to school one day,
Which was against the rule;
It made the children laugh and play
To see a lamb at school.

It   followed   her   to   school   one   day,

Which   was   against   the   rule;

It   made   the   children   laugh   and   play

To   see   a   lamb   at   school.

RAIN

Rain, rain, go away,
Come again some other day;
Little Johnny wants to play.

Rain,   rain,   go   away,

Come   again   some   other   day;

Little   Johnny   wants   to   play.

JACK BE NIMBLE

Jack be nimble, Jack be quick,
Jack jump over the candle stick.

| Jack | be | nimble, | Jack | be | quick. |

| Jack | jump | over | the | candle | stick. |

Twinkle, Twinkle Little Star

Twinkle, twinkle, little star,
How I wonder what you are!

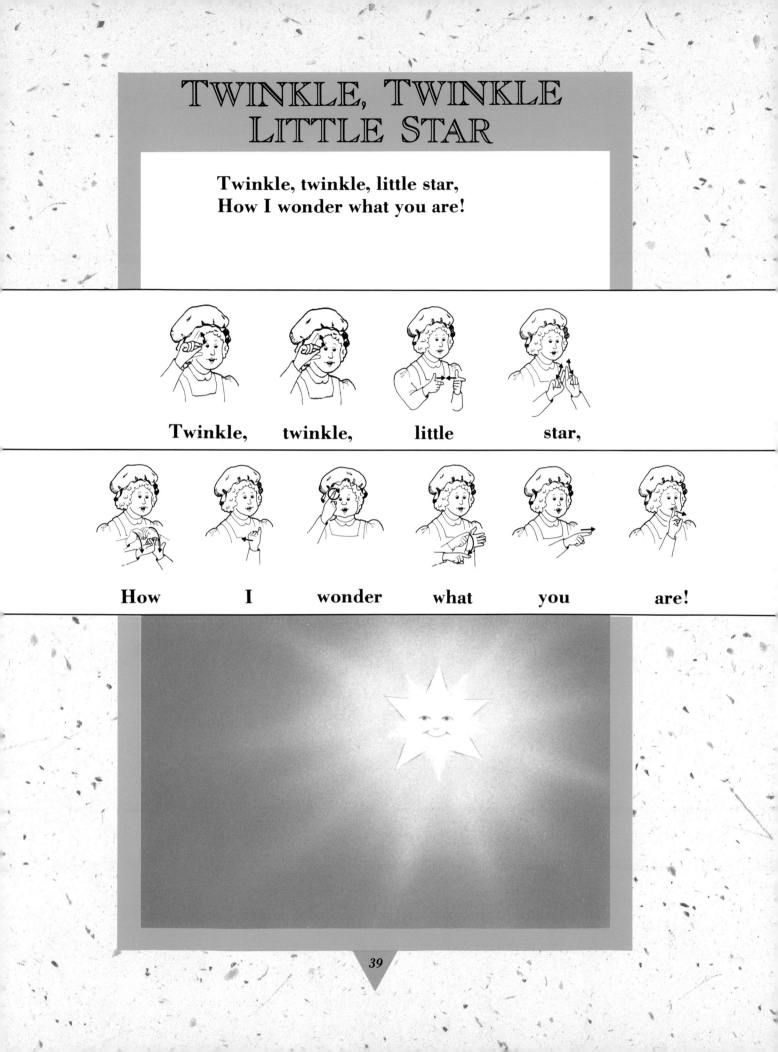

Twinkle,   twinkle,   little   star,

How   I   wonder   what   you   are!

Up above the world so high,
Like a diamond in the sky.
Twinkle, twinkle, little star,
How I wonder what you are!

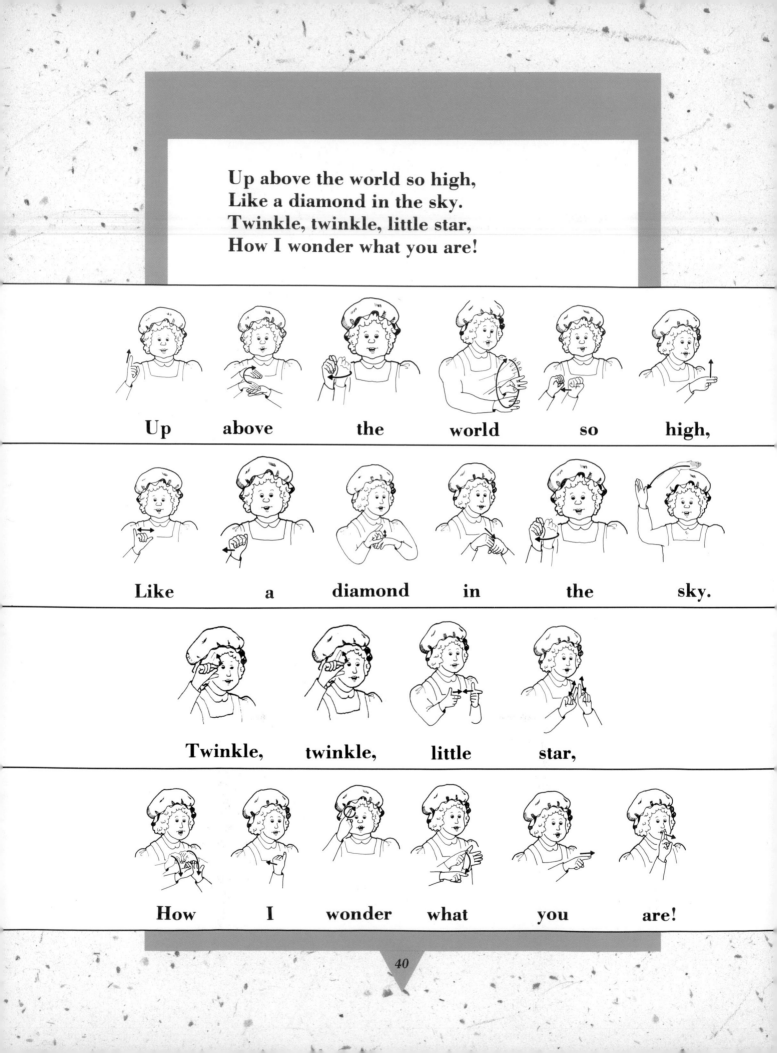

Up   above   the   world   so   high,

Like   a   diamond   in   the   sky.

Twinkle,   twinkle,   little   star,

How   I   wonder   what   you   are!